KID GUARDIAN

Planet Earth Patrol

TM

SERIES

What's Happening to the Rain Forests?

by
Richard D. Covey
& Diane H. Pappas

Illustrated by
The Pixel Factory

SCHOLASTIC INC.
New York Toronto London Auckland Sydney
Mexico City New Delhi Hong Kong Buenos Aires

To Uncle Nikos, Carson, and Brynne for caring for our planet
and someday visiting the rain forest.
—DHP & RDC

Special thanks to the talented artists of The Pixel Factory:
Willie Castro, Desma Thompson, & Bob Duane

ISBN-13: 978-0-545-06103-2
ISBN-10: 0-545-06103-2

Text and illustrations copyright © 2009 by A G Education, Inc.

12 11 10 9 8 7 6 5 4 3 2 1   9 10 11 12 13 14/0

Printed in the U.S.A.
First printing, March 2009

Note to parents and teachers: Please read this page to your children and students to introduce them to the Kid Guardians.

MEET THE KID GUARDIANS

From their home base in the mystical Himalayan mountain kingdom of Shambala, Zak the Yak and the Kid Guardians are always on alert, ready to protect the children of the world from danger.

ZAK THE YAK is a gentle giant with a heart of gold. He's the leader of the Kid Guardians.

Loyal and lovable, **SCRUBBER** is Zak's best friend and sidekick.

BUZZER is both street-smart and book-smart, with a real soft spot for kids.

Always curious about the world, **SMOOCH** loves to meet new people and see new places.

CARROT, with her wild red hair, is funny, lovable, and the first to jump in when help is needed.

Whenever a child is in danger, the **TROUBLE BUBBLE**™ sounds an alarm and then instantly transports the Kid Guardians to that location.

"Wow, Ms. Norman, what's happened to our classroom?" exclaimed Amanda. "It's so beautiful."
"Jesse's mom and I decorated it to show you what a rain forest looks like," replied Ms. Norman.

"What's so important about a big old jungle?" Jesse asked.
"It's just a bunch of trees, bugs, and poisonous snakes."
"Jesse," Ms. Norman replied, "we all need to understand how
important the rain forests are."

Meanwhile, back at Kid Guardian Headquarters . . .

"Let's go," shouted Zak. "Ms. Norman will be happy to see us."
"Hold on one second," said Carrot, "I'm going to bring Felix."

"Hi, Zak. Class, say hello to Carrot and Zak the Yak, leader of the Kid Guardians," said Ms. Norman. "Thanks for coming to help us. Carrot, I see you've brought Felix, too."

"Yes," said Carrot, "he's my pet tree frog from the rain forest."

"Jesse, you asked why the rain forests are so important," Zak said. "Well, the best way to learn is to visit one. The Trouble Bubble will have us there and back in no time."

"We are going to visit the biggest rain forest in the world, the Amazon rain forest. It is so big, it crosses over four South American countries — Brazil, Venezuela, Colombia, and Ecuador," explained Zak.

"That's the 4,000-mile-long Amazon River. It provides water the rain forest needs to live," said Zak. "People call rain forests the 'lungs' of our planet. They keep the air on Earth fresh by recycling carbon dioxide into oxygen."

"More than half of the world's 10 million types of plants, animals, and insects live in the rain forest," Carrot explained. "And about 2,000 different types of frogs, like Felix!"

"Wow! This is amazing. Please show us more," said Jesse.

"More than 3,000 different fruits and vegetables, such as bananas, avocados, and coconuts, come from the rain forest," said Carrot. "Also, lots of medicines we use today come from plants in the rain forest. And don't forget chocolate!"

"The rain forests are more than 80 million years old,"
Carrot added. "We all must help protect the rain forests.
People are cutting down the trees to make things like paper
products or lumber for houses."

"I want you to see what happens when too many trees are cut down," Zak said. "All the plants and animals disappear. By learning about the rain forest you can take better care of it."

"Gee, Zak, now I understand why rain forests are important and need protection," Jesse said.

"That's great, Jesse!" said Zak. "We hope that you, and kids like you, will spread the news about the importance of rain forests to all of your friends."

"Kids," said Zak, "if you can help others understand the need to protect the rain forests, you can help save them."

1. Rain forests are home to thousands of plants and animals.
2. Rain forests help make fresh air and stabilize the world's climate.
3. Rain forests help protect against flood, drought, and erosion.
4. Rain forests are a source of medicines and foods.